THIS WHERE'S WALDO? BOOK BELONGS TO:

_____

_____

HEY, WALDO FANS! FIVE INTREPID TRAVELERS ARE LOST IN EVERY SCENE! CAN YOU FIND THEM?

ODLAW   WIZARD WHITEBEARD   WENDA   WOOF   WALDO

AND IN EVERY SCENE, THE TRAVELERS HAVE EACH LOST SOMETHING PRECIOUS! CAN YOU FIND THESE ITEMS TOO?

WALDO'S KEY   WOOF'S BONE   WENDA'S CAMERA

WIZARD WHITEBEARD'S SCROLL   ODLAW'S BINOCULARS

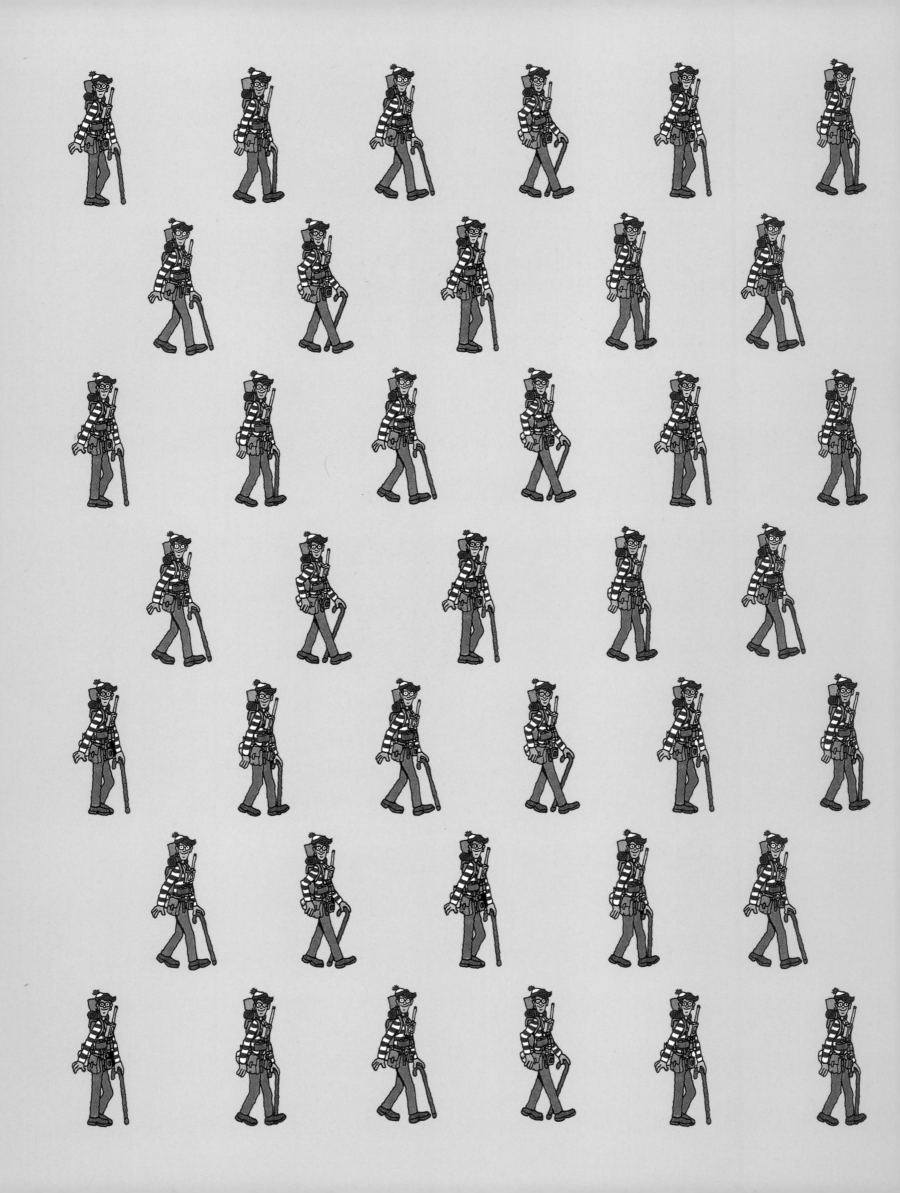

For Waldo

Copyright © 1987–2017 by Martin Handford

All rights reserved. No part of this book may be reproduced, transmitted, or stored in an
information retrieval system in any form or by any means, graphic, electronic, or mechanical,
including photocopying, taping, and recording, without prior written permission from the publisher.

First U.S. paperback edition 2017

Library of Congress Cataloging-in-Publication Data is available.

Library of Congress Catalog Card Number 97014990

ISBN 978-0-7636-4525-0 (hardcover)
ISBN 978-0-7636-3498-8 (paperback)
ISBN 978-0-7636-9579-8 (30th anniversary edition)

19 20 21 WKT 35 34

Printed in Shenzhen, Guangdong, China

This book was typeset in Optima and Wallyfont.
The illustrations were done in watercolor and water-based ink.

Candlewick Press
99 Dover Street
Somerville, Massachusetts 02144

visit us at www.candlewick.com

MARTIN HANDFORD

CANDLEWICK PRESS

HI, FRIENDS!

MY NAME IS WALDO. I'M JUST SETTING OFF ON A WORLDWIDE HIKE. YOU CAN COME TOO. ALL YOU HAVE TO DO IS FIND ME.

I'VE GOT ALL I NEED—WALKING STICK, KETTLE, MALLET, CUP, BACKPACK, SLEEPING BAG, BINOCULARS, CAMERA, SNORKEL, BELT, BAG, AND SHOVEL.

I'M NOT TRAVELING ON MY OWN. WHEREVER I GO, THERE ARE LOTS OF OTHER CHARACTERS FOR YOU TO SPOT. FIRST FIND WOOF (BUT ALL YOU CAN SEE IS HIS TAIL), WENDA, WIZARD WHITEBEARD, AND ODLAW. THEN FIND 25 WALDO-WATCHERS SOMEWHERE, EACH OF WHOM APPEARS ONLY ONCE IN MY TRAVELS. CAN YOU FIND ONE OTHER CHARACTER WHO APPEARS IN EVERY SCENE? ALSO IN EVERY SCENE, CAN YOU SPOT MY KEY, WOOF'S BONE, WENDA'S CAMERA, WIZARD WHITEBEARD'S SCROLL, AND ODLAW'S BINOCULARS?

WOW! WHAT A SEARCH!   Waldo

GREETINGS, WALDO-FOLLOWERS! WOW, THE BEACH WAS GREAT TODAY! ALL AROUND ME I SAW STRIPES ON TOWELS, CLOTHES, UMBRELLAS, AND BEACH HUTS. THERE WAS A SAND CASTLE WITH A REAL KNIGHT IN ARMOR INSIDE! FANTASTIC!

Waldo

WHERE'S WALDO? ON THE BEACH

TO:
WALDO-FOLLOWERS
HERE, THERE,
EVERYWHERE

STEP RIGHT UP, WALDO-FUN LOVERS! I'VE LOST ALL MY THINGS, ONE IN EVERY PLACE I'VE VISITED. GO BACK AND FIND THEM! AND SOMEWHERE ONE OF THE WALDO-WATCHERS HAS LOST A POM-POM FROM HIS HAT. CAN YOU SPOT WHICH ONE, AND FIND THE MISSING POM-POM?

NOW KEEP GOING! FROM HERE THERE'S ONE FINAL STOP ON MY JOURNEY, BACK IN TOWN AGAIN! BUT A LOT HAS CHANGED THERE. CAN YOU SPOT ALL THE DIFFERENCES AND FIND WHERE EVERYTHING NEW HAS COME FROM?

Waldo

WHERE FAIRGROUND WALDO?

TO:
WALDO-FUN LOVERS,
ROUND AND ROUND,
TWIST AND TURN,
LOOP-THE-LOOP

THE GREAT WHERE'S WALDO? CHECKLIST
Hundreds more things for Waldo-watchers to watch out for!

IN TOWN

- A dog on a roof
- A man on a fountain
- A man about to trip over a dog's leash
- A car crash
- A happy barber
- People on a sidewalk watching television
- A puncture caused by an arrow
- A tearful tune
- A boy attacked by a plant
- A sandwich
- A waiter who isn't concentrating
- Two firefighters waving at each other
- A face on a wall
- A man coming out of a manhole
- A man feeding birds

SKI SLOPES

- A man reading on a roof
- A flying skier
- A runaway skier
- A backward skier
- A portrait in snow
- An illegal fisherman
- Five people wearing striped scarves
- Snow about to fall on two laughing men
- Three skiers who have hit trees
- An alpenhorn
- Two broken flagpoles
- A flag collector
- Four people in yellow-hooded tops
- A skier up a tree
- A water-skier on snow
- A yeti
- Two skiing reindeer
- A roof jumper
- Someone crashing through five skiers

THE TRAIN STATION

- Four shovels and five spades
- A trolley carrying five suitcases
- People being knocked over by a door
- A man about to step on a ball
- Three different times at the same time
- A wheelbarrow baby carriage
- A face on a train
- Five people reading one newspaper
- A show-off with a suitcase
- Someone tripping over a dog
- Two men with red-and-white-striped ties
- A smoking train
- A squeeze on a bench
- A dog tearing a man's pants
- A man sitting on a suitcase
- Twenty cows
- Someone desperately trying to lift a suitcase
- Two suitcases spilling their contents
- A broken weighing machine

ON THE BEACH

- A dog and its owners wearing sunglasses
- A man who is overdressed
- A muscular man with a medal
- A water-skier
- A striped photographer
- A punctured air mattress
- A donkey who likes ice cream
- A man being squashed
- A punctured beach ball
- A human pyramid
- Three people reading newspapers
- A cowboy
- A human donkey
- A radio
- An irritated human stepping-stone
- A red air mattress
- Age and beauty
- Two red-and-yellow umbrellas
- Two men in tank tops, one without
- A sand-castle show-off
- Someone wearing suspenders
- A cream-colored dog
- Three protruding tongues
- Two oddly fitting hats
- Five sprinters
- A towel with a hole in it
- A punctured hovercraft
- A boy who's not allowed any ice cream
- Two caps with extra-long peaks

CAMPSITE

- A bull in a hedge
- Bullhorns
- A shark in the canal
- A bull seeing red
- A careless kick
- Tea in a lap
- A low bridge
- A person knocked over by a mallet
- A man surprised undressing
- A bicycle tire about to be punctured
- Six dogs
- An ineffective scarecrow
- A teepee
- Large biceps
- Three campers with very long beards
- A collapsed tent
- A smoking barbecue
- A fisherman catching old boots
- An old-fashioned bicycle
- A Boy Scout making fire
- A roller hiker
- A man blowing up a raft
- Thirsty walkers
- Runners on the road
- A bull chasing two people
- A campers' butler

AIRPORT

- A flying saucer
- A boy sitting with the revolving luggage
- A leaking fuel pipe
- Flight controllers playing badminton
- A rocket
- A tower on top of the control tower
- Three watch smugglers
- An airport worker resting on a plane
- A forklift
- A wind sock
- Someone with a bucket and shovel
- Six stewardesses in light-blue uniforms
- A plane with giant tail wings
- A fire engine and ten firefighters
- Two passengers wearing white hats
- A plane that doesn't fly
- A flying ace
- A pen and paper
- Runners on a runway
- Five men blowing up a balloon
- Dracula
- Three childish pilots
- Eighteen airport workers with yellow caps

SPORTS STADIUM

- Three pairs of feet, sticking out of the sand
- A cowboy starting races
- Hopeless hurdlers
- Records being thrown by a discus thrower
- A shot-put juggler
- An ear trumpet
- A vaulting horse
- A runner with two wheels
- A parachuting vaulter
- A Scotsman running with a caber
- An elephant pulling a rope
- People being knocked over by a hammer
- A gardener
- Three frogmen
- A runner without any shorts on
- A bed
- A bandaged boy
- A runner with four legs
- A sunken jumper
- Two athletes with striped towels
- A boy squirting water
- Ten children taking part in the three-legged race
- A referee chasing a dog chasing a cat chasing a mouse

AT SEA

- A windsurfer
- A raft punctured by an arrow
- A sword fight with a swordfish
- A school of whales
- Seasick sailors
- A leaking diver
- A bathtub
- A bearded man wearing sunglasses
- A game of tic-tac-toe
- A lucky fisherman
- Three lumberjacks
- Unlucky fishermen
- Two water-skiers in a tangle
- A cowboy riding a sea horse
- Fish robbers
- A fishy photo
- Uninvited pirates climbing aboard the cruise ship
- A Chinese junk
- A wave at sea
- A man being strangled by an octopus
- A boat that has crashed into a safety buoy

DEPARTMENT STORE

- A red-suited stroller passenger
- A man whose boots face the wrong way
- A man with heavy packages
- A misbehaving vacuum cleaner
- Ties that match their wearers
- A baby carriage bumping into a shopper
- A boy trying on a top hat
- A man trying on a jacket that's too big
- A girl wearing a red hooded sweatshirt
- A boy riding in a shopping cart
- A dangerous glove that's come alive
- A shopper tripping over a ball on the floor

FAIRGROUND

- A cannon at a rifle range
- A bumper car run wild
- Ten colored hoops
- A one-armed bandit
- A doll
- Twelve uniformed fairground staff
- A runaway merry-go-round horse
- Six birds
- A haunted house
- Seven lost children and a lost dog
- A tank crash
- Three clowns
- Three men dressed as bears

MUSEUM

- A very big skeleton
- A clown squirting water
- A boy in a catapult
- A bird's nest in a woman's hair
- A popping bicep
- One circular portrait picture frame
- A knight watching television
- Picture robbers
- A toppling row of pots
- A highwayman
- A leaking watercolor
- Fighting pictures
- A king and queen
- A rude character inside a picture
- Three cavemen
- A woman wearing a red scarf
- Charioteers
- A collapsing pillar

SAFARI PARK

- Noah's ark
- A message in a bottle
- A hippo having its teeth cleaned
- A bird's nest in an antler
- A hungry giraffe
- An ice-cream robber
- Zebras crossing
- Santa Claus and a contented reindeer
- A unicorn
- Fifteen park rangers
- Papa Bear, Mama Bear, and Baby Bear
- Caged people
- A lion driving a car
- Tarzan
- Lion Cubs Scouts
- Two women with red handbags
- Two lines for the bathrooms
- Animals' beauty parlor
- An elephant squirting water

IN TOWN AGAIN!

- A rhinoceros on a roof
- Three backpackers on a plane
- A lion sitting at a desk
- A bumper car driving on the road
- An elephant leaving the barbershop
- Two anchored ropes
- An arrow in a wall
- A rooftop barbecue
- A mermaid waving at a dog
- A clown portrait being admired
- A giraffe coming out of a manhole
- A seagull eating a truckload of fish

WOW! WHAT A SEARCH!

Did you find Waldo, all his friends, and all the things they lost? Did you find the one scene where Waldo and Odlaw both lost their binoculars? Odlaw's binoculars are the ones nearest to him. Did you find the extra character who appears in every scene? If not, keep looking!
Wow! Fantastic!

AND JUST ONE MORE THING . . .

The search continues! Did you find the one character from In Town Again! who is not in any other scene?

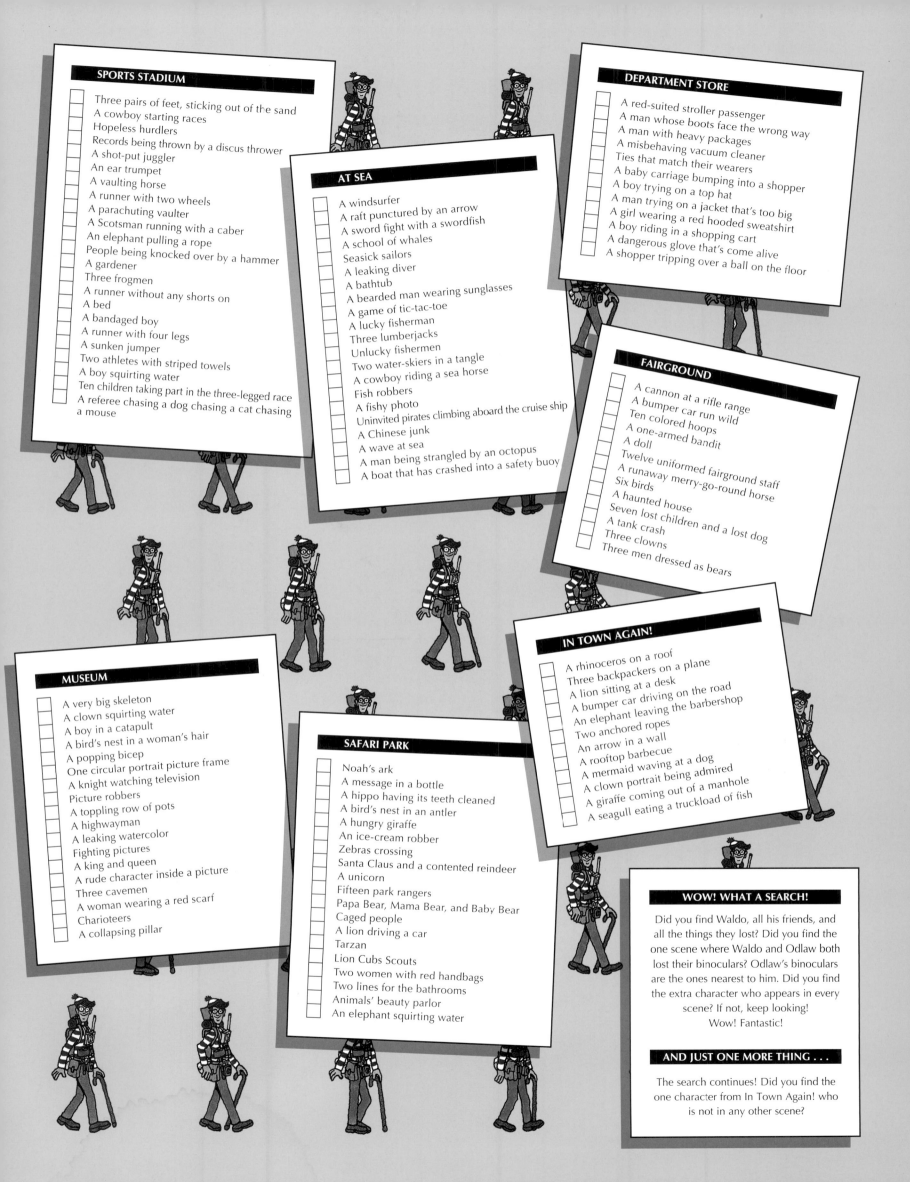

TO MY WALDO FANS AROUND THE WORLD,

THANK YOU FOR JOINING ME ON MY AMAZING ADVENTURES! DESTINATION HERE, THERE, AND EVERYWHERE IS MY MOTTO! I'M ALWAYS ON THE LOOKOUT FOR EXCITING PLACES TO EXPLORE THAT ARE TEEMING WITH CROWDS OF INTERESTING PEOPLE OR CHAOTIC CREATURES. I HOPE YOU HAVE ENJOYED TRAVELING ALL OVER THE GLOBE WITH ME TO FIND THEM. IT'S BEEN A BLAST! YOU'VE DEFINITELY EARNED YOUR RED-AND-WHITE STRIPES!

NOW IT'S TIME TO CELEBRATE 30 YEARS OF SEARCHING! LET'S HAVE SOME FUN! WEAR YOUR STRIPES LOUD AND PROUD WITH ME, WOOF, WENDA, WIZARD WHITEBEARD, AND ODLAW, AS WELL AS MY TRUSTY TROUPE OF 25 WALDO-WATCHERS.

THE ENJOYMENT DOESN'T STOP THERE! LOOK AT ALL OF THE CHARACTERS WALKING OUT OF THE STAMPS ON THIS LETTER! WOW! AREN'T THEY MARVELOUS! CAN YOU FIND FIFTEEN OF THEM ELSEWHERE IN THIS BOOK?

SEARCH FOR AMUSEMENT AND WONDER WHEREVER YOU GO! HAPPY HUNTING!

Waldo